THE CLASS PET FROM THE
BLACK LAGOON

STORY BY
MIKE THALER

PICTURES BY
JARED LEE

CLASS
PET

Cartwheel
·B·O·O·K·S·®

SCHOLASTIC INC.

New York   Toronto   London   Auckland   Sydney
Mexico City   New Delhi   Hong Kong   Buenos Aires

To the wonderful students at Cherokee Elementary and to their loving librarian, Michelle Sisk, and their principal, Mrs. Elizabeth Spurlock.—M.T.
For Buster, Shane, Brucey, Boots, Ginger, and Spanky... all dear companions past and present—J.L.

visit us at www.abdopublishing.com

Reinforced library bound edition published in 2014 by Spotlight, a division of the ABDO Group, PO Box 398166, Minneapolis, MN 55439. Spotlight produces high-quality reinforced library bound editions for schools and libraries. Published by agreement with Scholastic, Inc.

Printed in the United States of America, North Mankato, Minnesota.
102013
012014
This book contains at least 10% recycled materials.

Library of Congress Cataloging-in-Publication Data

This title was previously cataloged with the following information:

Thaler, Mike, 1936-
  The class pet from the Black Lagoon / by Mike Thaler ; pictures by Jared Lee
  p. cm. -- (Black Lagoon)
  Summary: Just how scary will the new class pet be? The class let's their imaginations run wild!
  1. Fear--Fiction. 2. Schools--Fiction. 3. Pets--Fiction. 4. First day of school--Fiction. I. Title. II Series.
PZ7.T3 Ckm 2003
[E]--dc23   2004540938

ISBN 978-1-61479-195-9 (Reinforced Library Bound Edition)

All Spotlight books are reinforced library binding
and manufactured in the United States of America.

Mrs. Green is bringing in a class pet.
She won't tell us what it is.

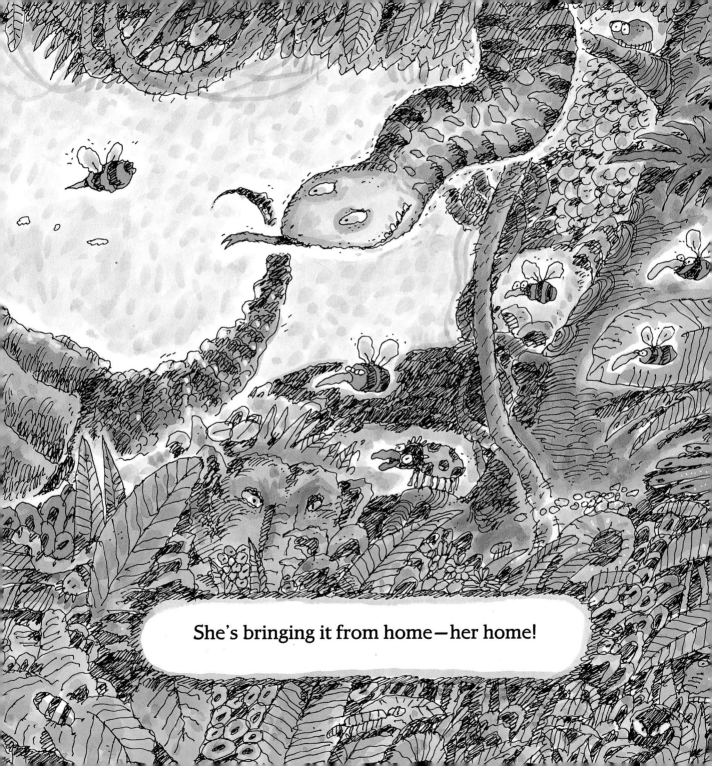

She's bringing it from home—her home!

I wonder what it will look like.
Will it have spots?

Will it have stripes?
Will it have splotches?

Will it have feathers?

Will it have fur?

Will it have scales?
Will it have horns?

Will it have headlights?

Will it hop? Will it jump?

Or will it just sit there like a lump?

Mrs. Green says she's bringing a cage, too!

Don't lions live in cages?

Will it be wild?

Will it be mild?

Can we pet it?
Can we hold it?

Can we take it for a walk?

And what will it eat? Lettuce? Custard? Us?
Maybe it will be a *carnivore*… and eat cars!

How many legs will it have? And how many teeth?
Two, four, six, eight... what will we appreciate?

Maybe it will be two animals stuck together like a *kangarooster*...

...or a *camelephant*!

Maybe it will be a big bug or just a big blob.

I'm scared!

Mrs. Green says its first name is Dina.

I hope its last name isn't *Saur*.

Well, here they come.

Two shadows cover the door.

In steps Mrs. Green with a hamster.

It doesn't look too ferocious.
In fact, it looks as scared as we looked.

I'm going to hug it and let it know that it
doesn't have anything to be afraid of.